To celebrate the "Big Birthday Year"
of Jo and Brian — Nana and Grandad
— much loved by Hannah, Maddy,
Clara, Abigail, Benjamin, and
Jake — and by me, of course
P. D.E.

For Lily Grace, with love D.A.

Sandy Creek
NEW YORK

An Imprint of Sterling Publishing
387 Park Avenue South
New York, NY 10016

SANDY CREEK and the distinctive Sandy Creek logo
are registered trademarks of Barnes & Noble, Inc.

Text © 2010 by Pamela Duncan Edwards
Illustrations © 2010 by Deborah Allwright

This 2013 edition published by Sandy Creek.

ISBN 978-1-4351-4923-6

Manufactured in China
Lot #:
2 4 6 8 10 9 7 5 3 1
08/13

Pamela Duncan Edwards

Dinosaur Sleepover

illustrated by Deborah Allwright

Sandy Creek
NEW YORK

What would you do if it was your cousin's birthday and he invited you and Dinosaur to a sleepover party?
What if Dinosaur looked puzzled?

You'd say, "We'll all have fun at the party, Dinosaur. Then everyone gets to stay overnight."

What if Dinosaur shook his handsome dinosaur head and said in a firm voice, "A dinosaur can't stay overnight because his family would miss him too much."

You'd say, "That's okay, Dinosaur, we can ask Pickles to look after our family while we're gone."

What if Dinosaur tapped his sparkling
dinosaur teeth and said in an anxious voice,
"Dinosaurs have to brush their teeth before
they go to bed. I wouldn't have my toothbrush
with me."

You'd say, "That's no problem, Dinosaur. We'll take our things in your stripy travel kit and we'll put your toothbrush in the pocket on the side."

What if Dinosaur blinked his bright dinosaur eyes and said in a worried voice, "If a dinosaur **did** go visiting, he'd have to take clean pajamas. My pajamas are in the washer!"

You'd say, "But you've got two pairs of pajamas, Dinosaur. Your other pair is folded and ready to pack."

What if Dinosaur made himself very small and said in a nervous voice,

"I'm afraid they'll forget to come for us in the morning. What if we have to sleep over forever and ever?"

You'd give Dinosaur a huge hug and say,
"I tell you what, Dinosaur, we'll write a big
note and stick it on the fridge. We'll say . . .

I bet that Dinosaur would wrinkle his bony dinosaur forehead,

and think very hard . . .

Then he'd say, "Okay!"
And off you'd go.

What if you were walking up the path to the
party and Dinosaur gave a gasp and cried,

"I didn't bring Teddy! A dinosaur
can't sleep without his teddy."

You'd laugh and say, "Silly old Dinosaur.
You put Teddy in your special bag.
His head is poking out of the top."

And I bet Dinosaur
would laugh, too.

What if you opened the door to the
party and everyone said,

"HELLO!"

I bet Dinosaur would smile his huge, toothy dinosaur smile and run to join the games.

Then you'd all play
musical chairs

and hide-and-seek

and catch the dinosaur's tail.

And lots of other games, until the birthday cake arrived.

And after your cousin had blown out all the candles, I bet Dinosaur would eat a **DINO-SIZED** piece of cake!

When it was time for bed, I bet
everyone would chatter and giggle

and maybe have a pillow fight.

Then you'd laugh and laugh until you were
all so tired you just had to go to sleep.

What if you were snuggled deep
down in your sleeping bag and Dinosaur
whispered in his happy dinosaur voice,
"When it's our birthday, should we
have a sleepover party?"

Then I bet you'd say,
"Great idea, Dinosaur!"